Might goes hand in hand with right as He-Man and the Masters of the Universe fight to make their planet safe. The greatest of their enemies is Skeletor, the Lord of Destruction, and his evil band, whose hatred for their foes is never-ending. The war goes on but who will win?

British Library Cataloguing in Publication Data

Grant, John, *1930-*
   He-Man and the Asteroid of Doom. —
   (Masters of the universe)
   I. Title   II. Davies, Robin, *1950-*
   III. Series
   823'.914[J]   PZ7

   ISBN 0-7214-0982-2

First edition

Published by Ladybird Books Ltd Loughborough Leicestershire UK
Ladybird Books Inc Lewiston Maine 04240 USA

david

![MASTERS OF THE UNIVERSE]

He-Man and the
Asteroid of Doom

by John Grant
illustrated by Robin Davies

Ladybird Books

He-Man and Man-at-Arms stood talking on the battlements of Castle Grayskull. "It has been very peaceful, lately," said Man-at-Arms.

"Too peaceful," replied He-Man. "We've had no trouble from Skeletor or any of his evil band. It doesn't seem right, somehow."

Teela joined them. "What a beautiful day," she said, looking up at the blue sky. "When I was a child, people used to say that Eternia's doom was in the sky. What did they mean?"

"Thousands of years ago," said Man-at-Arms, "the men of Eternia built a power system that would serve all of Eternia for ever — but they could not control it. So, the wise men ordered a huge rocket to be built. The power system was loaded aboard and the rocket was fired off towards the sun, where they expected that the deadly power system would be destroyed."

"And was it?" asked He-Man.

"The rocket collided with an asteroid not far above the surface of Eternia," said Man-at-Arms. "Fragments of the rocket are still believed to be in orbit out there. And the deadly power system may still be active."

At that very moment, far away in Etheria, Hordak was raging at members of the Horde. "Power!" he cried. "That is what I need! Power for weapons against the Rebels. There is not enough power in the whole of Etheria for my needs!"

Modulok had been listening. Now, he sidled up to Hordak and hissed, "I have heard of a source of power, more than you will ever need."

"Where is it? Why was I not told of this before?" snarled Hordak.

"It is far away," hissed Modulok. "In the asteroid belt which encircles Eternia there is one particular asteroid. Anyone who can take possession of it will have the greatest source of power in the entire galaxy."

The other members of the Horde laughed.

"The Asteroid of Power!" cried Grizzlor. "Everyone knows that it is only a fairy tale!"

"Fairy tale or not," said Hordak, "I intend to investigate. We leave at once for Eternia. If there is such a thing as the Asteroid of Power, then I will have it!"

Before the day was out, Hordak and the Horde were aboard their intergalactic space cruiser. A fleet of Fliers was loaded into the cargo hold. Each was equipped with a strong winch and cable.

The space cruiser blasted off from Etheria. On course for Eternia, the ship was put on automatic pilot. Then Hordak called a council of war.

"This will be a dangerous task," he said. "We first of all have to find the asteroid. Our instruments will help."

"How big is it?" asked Mantenna.

"Enormous," said Hordak. "Bigger than our cruiser. It will look like a small planet. The Fliers have been fitted with cables and magnetic clamps. Mantenna, Grizzlor, and Leech will take one each. I shall be in the fourth. We will attach cables to the asteroid and haul it out of orbit around Eternia. The space cruiser will tow it back to Etheria."

"What if Skeletor has got there first?" asked Grizzlor. "It's nearer his base in Snake Mountain."

"That blundering fool has not the brain for such a task," cried Hordak. "And, in that case, I should have heard from my spies."

When Hordak's craft was close to the asteroid
zone, it appeared on the radar screens at Castle
Grayskull. The Masters of the Universe watched
as it drew closer. Then it stopped, just beyond
the asteroids.

"Is it an enemy?" asked Teela.

"I can't say," said He-Man. "But friendly
visitors do not usually skulk out in space. Let's
call them up."

But there was no reply to radio messages from Castle Grayskull. He-Man listened to the crackle of static. "And friendly visitors are also usually glad to make conversation," he said. "This wants looking into."

"Could it be that Skeletor is up to something?" said Man-at-Arms.

"There's one way to find out," said Teela. "Keep watch on him. Where's Buzz-Off?"

Soon, the winged look-out was hovering high above Snake Mountain. But he reported no sign of anything suspicious.

Although Buzz-Off had seen nothing from the
air, Skeletor was very busy indeed beneath
Snake Mountain. He too knew that a strange
space craft was hovering just beyond Eternia's
asteroid zone. Skeletor thought of everyone as an
enemy. Whoever was out there must be
destroyed, before they destroyed him. He sent
Zodac in a small space-scout craft to investigate.

Zodac blasted off and made for the asteroid zone, then wove his way carefully through the circling asteroids. And there, beyond the outermost asteroid, was a huge, black space cruiser. Clearly visible on the side was the evil, bat-winged symbol of Hordak.

Zodac quickly took cover among the asteroids. Then he switched on his radio receiver. Hordak's voice came crackling through. Zodac could tell that he was issuing orders to his warriors, but that was all. Just what Hordak was planning to do, it was impossible to make out.

Zodac set course back to Snake Mountain, radioing his report to Skeletor as he went — and in Castle Grayskull, the Masters of the Universe picked up that message.

13

"This is serious," said He-Man. "Hordak would not come all the way from Etheria to Eternia for nothing. What can he possibly want, hanging about up there among the asteroids?"

"Perhaps he's planning to steal an asteroid," said Orko. "I've heard that Hordak will take anything that isn't nailed down."

"You know," said Man-at-Arms, "you may be right, Orko!"

"I'm sure I am," said Orko. "Hordak is very dishonest."

"Not *that*," said Man-at-Arms. "About the asteroid. There is only one asteroid worth stealing. Teela mentioned it the other day."

"Of course! The ancient power system! The Asteroid of Power! Some say that it is only a story. But if Hordak is after it... then it *must* be there!"

"For the sake of all Eternia," said He-Man, "the Masters of the Universe must stop him before it is too late!"

But the Masters of the Universe were not the only ones to guess what Hordak was up to. Skeletor had also heard the story of the Asteroid of Power. If anyone was going to seize it, *he* was going to be the one.

He set his slave technicians to the construction of a powerful magnetic beam projector. When it was finished, they hauled it up out of the depths and erected it on the highest point of Snake Mountain.

"All I have to do now," Skeletor cried with glee, "is to wait for Hordak to find the asteroid! Then, when he least expects it, my magnetic beam will pull it from his grasp. The greatest power source in all Eternia will be mine. I shall rule without hindrance from the Masters of the Universe or anybody else!"

Then he settled down to watch the radar screen, and await the moment to strike.

Out in space, Hordak was studying the
asteroid zone. The asteroids were of all shapes
and sizes. Some were simply jagged chunks of
rock broken from ancient planets. Others were
round, like small planets themselves. No one
could tell him what the Asteroid of Power was
likely to look like.

Mantenna took over the look-out.

Suddenly, he called out, "I see something!"

"The asteroid?" cried Hordak.

"No," replied Mantenna, "but it can't be far
away!"

18

Drifting past the windows of the space cruiser
were a number of things which did not look like
asteroids. There were pieces of twisted metal.
Broken frames. Fragments of machinery...
pieces of a giant rocket. And then, they saw it.
It must be the power unit. A great metal ball as
big as the cruiser. The metal was battered and
dented by meteorites. The cold of space had
cracked it in places. The heat of the sun had
scorched it. But there was no doubt: Hordak
had found the Asteroid of Power.

Quickly, Hordak issued his orders. The
warriors of the Horde raced to the cargo hold
where the fleet of special Fliers stood ready.
Mantenna, Grizzlor and Leech boarded their
craft. Hordak made a last check, then he
climbed into the Command Flier.

At a signal from Hordak, the outer doors of
the cargo hold swung slowly open. Then, with a
roar of jets, the four small craft zoomed out into
space.

The huge shape of the asteroid lay straight
ahead. The Fliers wheeled into formation. One
after the other they swooped close to the metal
surface. At the touch of a button a powerful,
magnetic clamp shot out. With a loud clang,

each clamp fastened itself to the asteroid. The
Fliers backed off, letting out cable as they went,
each cable attached to a clamp.

"Now!" cried Hordak over the radio. "FULL
POWER!"

The Fliers' jets spouted red flame. The cables
creaked. And very slowly the giant metal
asteroid began to move out of orbit.

At full power, the four small craft moved slowly. Their engines glowed red-hot. They shook with the strain. The cables were at breaking point. But still the asteroid was barely moving.

Then suddenly, there was a loud crash. Two of the clamps came loose. The Fliers spun out of control, almost colliding with Hordak and each other.

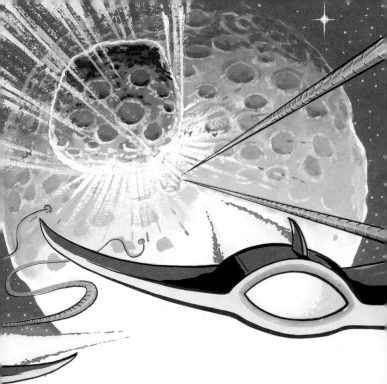

A small rocky asteroid had smashed into the metal one, which was already drifting back into orbit.

Hordak screamed over the radio, "RE-ENGAGE CLAMPS! RESUME TOW!"

Leech and Mantenna in their Fliers re-fixed their magnetic clamps. Once again the small craft took the strain.

And far below, on the surface of Eternia, Skeletor was preparing to take a hand!

On the summit of Snake Mountain, Skeletor adjusted the controls of his magnetic beam projector. Its sensors had located the asteroid. Skeletor watched the instruments as the asteroid drew closer in its orbit of the planet. "Stand by!" he ordered his slaves.

"FIVE, FOUR, THREE, TWO, ONE... ACTIVATE!"

A shimmering beam of magnetic energy shot into the sky from the machine. Skeletor watched the instruments again.

"We've made contact!" he cried. "Activate traction phase!"

Again a slave moved a control. A loud hum came from the machine.

In his Flier, Hordak felt himself being pulled back. He saw the asteroid bathed in a glowing energy field, and screamed at his warriors for full power. But it was useless. The asteroid was being drawn towards the surface of Eternia. One by one the magnetic clamps were pulled off as Hordak lost the tug-of-war with Skeletor.

Skeletor's magnetic beam projector drew the asteroid slowly out of orbit, and soon it could be seen from Eternia. From the battlements of Castle Grayskull, the Masters of the Universe looked up into the sky. The asteroid was a small, bright speck, but it grew bigger by the hour. Man-at-Arms sat at the Castle computer. "I have calculated that the asteroid is completely out of orbit," he said. "It will strike the surface of our planet late tomorrow."

"Where?" asked He-Man.

"Snake Mountain," replied Man-at-Arms.

"Oh, good!" cried Orko. "That will save everyone a great deal of trouble in the future."

"No," said He-Man. "We must try to stop it. There is certainly all manner of evil in Snake Mountain, but there are many innocent slaves and captives in Skeletor's dungeons."

"And," said Teela, "if what is said about the asteroid is true, it will not only destroy Snake Mountain, but much of the planet around."

"We have not a moment to waste if we are to stop it," said He-Man, leading the way to the parked Wind Raiders.

At full speed, the fleet of Wind Raiders raced
towards Snake Mountain, where Skeletor and his
evil band were clustered round the magnetic
beam projector. They only realised that
something was amiss when a blast of fire from
the Masters' laser cannons zipped about their
heads. As they dived for cover, Skeletor stood up
and shook his fist at the Wind Raiders.

He-Man brought his machine to hover above
the mountain. "Stop your magnetic beam
projector, Skeletor!" he cried. "You don't know
what you're doing!"

"I am taking possession of the mightiest power source in Eternia!" snarled back the Lord of Destruction.

"It will destroy you!" cried He-Man. "Switch off the projector!"

"Never!" cried Skeletor.

"In that case, the Masters of the Universe must do it for you!" cried He-Man. He put his Wind Raider into a steep, fast climb. Then, with the others in formation, he came in fast towards the projector, cannons blazing.

In a blinding flash of energy, Skeletor's magnetic beam projector exploded. As the pieces clattered to the ground and the smoke cleared, He-Man looked up to the sky. The asteroid was still there. But – would it stay where it was?

In the Wind Raiders as well as on Snake Mountain, all eyes were turned to the sky. The worst had happened. The Masters of the Universe had failed. They had destroyed Skeletor's equipment too late. The asteroid was coming closer and closer every moment!

"There's nothing more we can do here," said He-Man. And he led the others back to Castle Grayskull.

Once more, Man-at-Arms went to the computer. "The asteroid is moving faster," he reported. "Eternia's gravity is pulling it down. It is still headed for Snake Mountain."

"Call Skeletor on the radio," said He-Man. "Tell him to evacuate Snake Mountain at once."

"I don't think there's time for that," said Teela. "But if we can't stop the asteroid... could we divert it? Make it come down somewhere harmless?"

"Good thinking," said He-Man. "Our lasers might just do it."

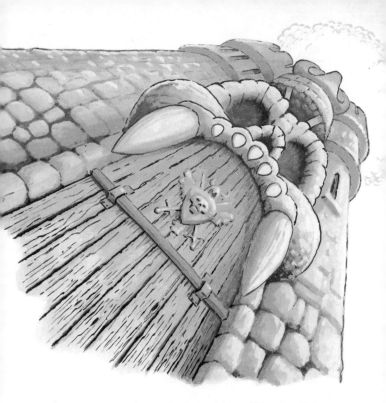

Once more the Wind Raiders lifted off from Castle Grayskull. Their energy packs were fully charged, and their laser cannons set at maximum thrust.

The asteroid was quite clear now. It glowed red as it hit the edge of Eternia's atmosphere.

Man-at-Arms had been doing some calculations on his on-board computer.

"If we can alter the course of the asteroid by fourteen and a half degrees," he reported, "it

will miss Snake Mountain and come down in the sea."

"But what if there are ships in that part?" said Teela.

"There won't be," said Man-at-Arms. "That part of the ocean is the Sea of Sargon. It is a mass of foul and poisonous weed. Nothing can pass through it. Nothing can live there."

"Right!" cried He-Man. "All Wind Raiders... maximum altitude!"

The Masters of the Universe levelled out
where the atmosphere of Eternia was thin, on
the edge of space itself. He-Man led them on a
course which would take them alongside the
asteroid. Once in position he gave the order:
"All lasers... FIRE!"

Instantly, there was a blaze of energy from
each Wind Raider. The asteroid kept straight
on!

Again the Masters of the Universe turned on the power of the laser cannons.

"It's turning!" called Teela. "I'm sure I saw it move!"

Another blast, and this time there was no mistake. The battered metal asteroid was swinging off in a new direction.

"Cease firing," ordered He-Man. "Man-at-Arms, how is it heading now?"

"Ten degrees," said Man-at-Arms. "That's not enough. It will hit the coast near several large towns. We must try again."

Then, Teela shouted a warning: "Look out! We have company!"

A fleet of Rotons had come skimming across the land below, and they were now climbing towards the Wind Raiders. At the controls could be clearly seen Skeletor, Zodac, Beast-Man, Evil-Lyn and others of Skeletor's evil band.

"As if we hadn't enough problems," said He-Man. "Stand by to repel attack!"

The Rotons swung round and opened fire with their energy weapons. But — not at the Wind Raiders! They were aiming, as the Masters of the Universe had done, at the speeding asteroid.

"Come on!" sounded Skeletor's voice over the radio. "Your puny efforts are useless. It needs me and my people for a job like this!"

"Right, Skeletor!" cried He-Man in a surprised voice. In a moment every laser cannon was turned on the asteroid. It swung further off course, and in a few minutes had crossed the coast, heading over the sea.

He-Man watched it go. "Thank you, Skeletor," he said. "There is some good in you after all!"

"Rubbish!" snarled Skeletor. "Do you think that I wanted that heap of scrap on top of Snake Mountain? What's more... if I can't have it, neither can Hordak!"

An evil voice came crackling over the radio. "Did someone mention my name?"

It was Hordak! Still determined to capture the Asteroid of Power, he had led his fleet of Fliers after it, following it into Eternia's atmosphere.

"Out of my way!" he snarled. His small craft shot past He-Man and Skeletor. The asteroid was now curving down for its final plunge into the sea beyond the horizon.

"Your stupidity nearly destroyed Snake Mountain, Hordak!" cried Skeletor, and he set off with his henchmen after Hordak. He-Man watched the Fliers disappear after the asteroid, and Skeletor's Rotons skim above the waves after the Fliers.

"We have done all we can," he said. "There's no way we can stop these two evil fools from destroying each other."

From a safe height, the Masters of the Universe waited to see what would happen.

Hordak and Skeletor were still screaming insults at each other when the asteroid hit the sea directly below them. It flew into a thousand pieces as it hit the water. A moment later, the ancient power system exploded in a blinding glare of energy.

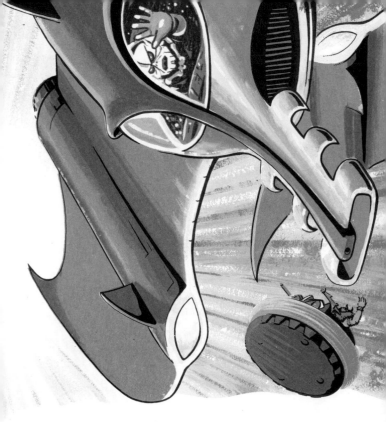

The Fliers and Rotons were thrown in all directions. A giant cloud of smoke and steam rose from the sea, and Hordak, Skeletor and their followers blundered about inside it. One by one the battered Fliers rose from the cloud and limped upwards towards the safety of the orbiting space cruiser.

Skeletor saw them go. Dazed, all *he* wanted to do was get back safely to Snake Mountain.

The Masters of the Universe watched the deadly mushroom cloud rising above the horizon. The blast caught the Wind Raiders even at that distance, tossing them about in the air like leaves.

As the cloud drifted away and disappeared, Teela said, "The planet of Eternia can sleep more safely now that danger has gone from the sky."

"Do you think that Skeletor and Hordak were destroyed with it?" said He-Man.

"That would be too much to expect," said Man-at-Arms. "I don't think that we have heard the last of either of them."

And they set off for Castle Grayskull, to await the next challenge for the Masters of the Universe.